Place **Busy Bee** on the red circles, then count the bees he leaves behind when he buzzes away!

Ten Buzzy Bees

By **Sally Crabtree**   Illustrated by **John Wallace**

David&Charles
Children's Books

Ten buzzy bees flying in a line . . .

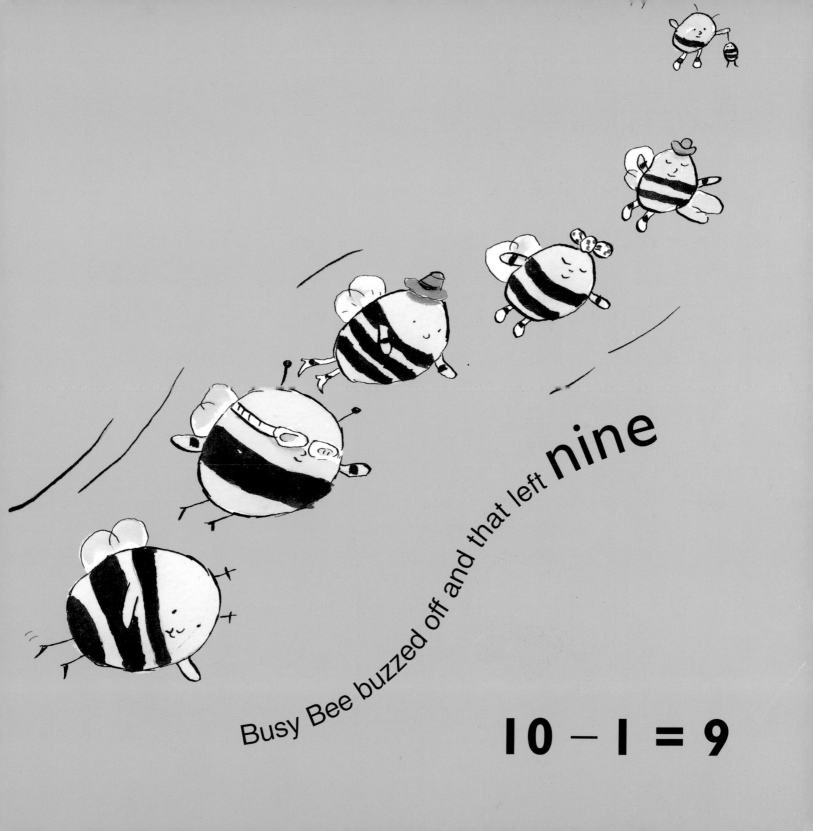

Busy Bee buzzed off and that left nine

10 − 1 = 9

Nine buzzy bees
Resting on a gate
Busy Bee buzzed off
And that left **eight**

$$9 - 1 = 8$$

Seven buzzy bees

Balancing on sticks

Busy Bee buzzed off

And that left six

$$7 - 1 = 6$$

Busy Bee buzzed off and that left five

6 − 1 = 5

Five buzzy bees

On the sticky floor

Busy Bee buzzed off

And that left **four**

$$5 - 1 = 4$$

Four buzzy bees

Hiding in a tree

Busy Bee buzzed off

And that left **three**

4 − 1 = 3

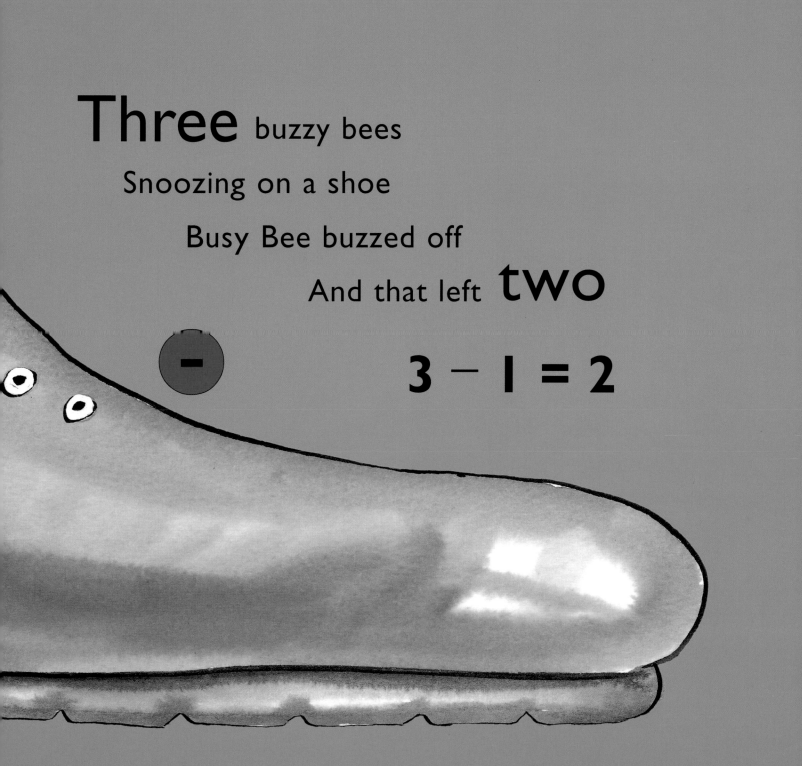

Three buzzy bees

Snoozing on a shoe

Busy Bee buzzed off

And that left **two**

$3 - 1 = 2$

Two buzzy bees
Dancing in the sun
Busy Bee buzzed off . . .

And that left **one**

2 − 1 = 1

One Busy Bee

Sneaks a lift home